MINECRAFT
WHERE'S THE ZOMBIE?
AND OTHER MOBS

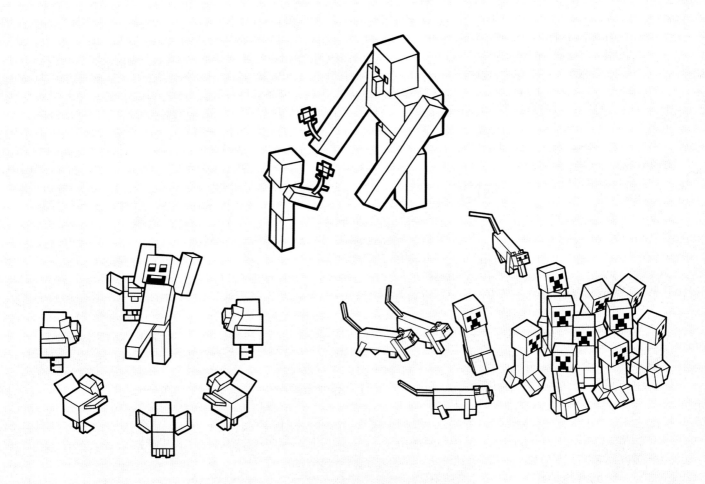

Random House 🏠 New York

© 2024 Mojang AB. All Rights Reserved. Minecraft, the Minecraft logo, the Mojang Studios logo and the Creeper
logo are trademarks of the Microsoft group of companies.
Published in the United States by Random House Children's Books, a division of Penguin Random House LLC,
1745 Broadway, New York, NY 10019, and in Canada by Penguin Random House Canada Limited, Toronto.
Random House and the colophon are registered trademarks of Penguin Random House LLC.
rhcbooks.com
minecraft.net
First published in Great Britain in 2024 by Farshore, an imprint of HarperCollins Publishers Limited.
First US edition published in 2025.
ISBN 978-0-593-80847-4 (trade)
MANUFACTURED IN CHINA
10 9 8 7 6 5 4 3 2 1

LOCATIONS

GROAN! Wait. What was that? GROAN! Argh, a zombie! Is there anywhere that is safe from them and their variants?

Five brave explorers have set out on separate adventures, but none of them have been seen for a while. Could the zombies have gotten them? Can you check in on all the explorers to make sure they're okay? Oh, and be sure to keep an eye out for those pesky zombies while you're at it!

FIND THE ZOMBIE

GET A MUSH-VROOM ON

TICK, TICK ... BOOM!

DISCOVER THE DROWNED

GETTING SOME VITAMIN SEA

A MONUMENT-OUS OCCASION

HUNT THE HUSK

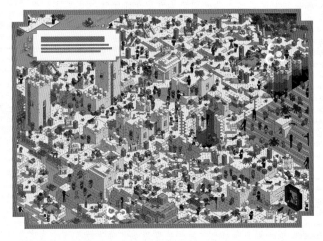

WE'LL NEVER DESERT YOU

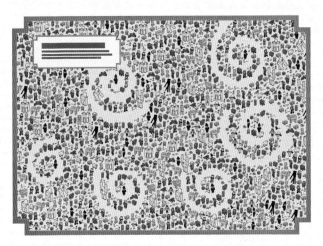

THE WICKED WITCH IS A PEST

DETECT THE ZOMBIE VILLAGER

PILLAGERS VS VILLAGERS

DAWN OF THE WELL-READ

SPOT THE ZOMBIFIED PIGLIN

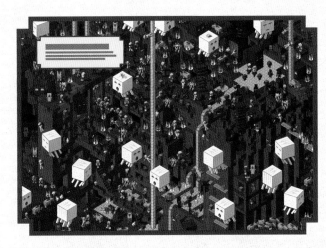

NEVER SAY NETHER

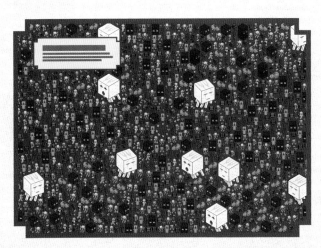

TAKE IT FOR A SPIN

FIND THE ZOMBIE

Bobby the Brave collects passive mobs for his zoo but gains many enemies on his way.

Bobby is currently on the hunt for a rare brown mooshroom and has heard rumors of one nearby. Armed with a lead and plenty of TNT, he has set out on an expedition to find this peculiar mob. However, with a zombie, creeper, and spider lurking in the shadows, will he survive the trip?

BOBBY THE BRAVE

Bobby is either very brave or very foolish. He is fascinated by all mobs, especially the creeper, whose explosive attacks he greatly admires. That's why instead of swords and bows, Bobby carries TNT for defense. The only issue is, Bobby doesn't have the stealth that the creeper has, and he sometimes forgets to run away before the TNT goes BOOM. Let's help Bobby find his mooshroom before TNT is needed.

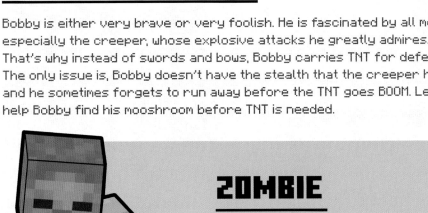

ZOMBIE

Though the sun is out, the dark forest and looming woodland mansion provide plenty of shade for zombies to survive the daytime. Can you spot this hostile mob hiding in the shadows?

BROWN MOOSHROOM

Bobby has many red mooshrooms in his zoo, but he longs to have a brown one. He did successfully breed one once, but he got peckish one day and decided to make mushroom stew. Little did he know that shearing the mushrooms off his brown mooshroom would turn it into a regular cow! He'll not make that mistake again!

CREEPER

HISS! Can you hear that? There's a creeper hiding somewhere, ready to pounce! BOOM! Wait, was that a creeper or Bobby? See if you can spot this sneaky mob before it finds Bobby and they enter into a TNT duel to the death. That won't end well for anyone!

SPIDER

Bobby needs to be careful of this mob. Though neutral in the daylight, it will turn hostile in the shade. Can you spot the spider and let Bobby know whether he should be worried?

GET A MUSH-VROOM ON

Bobby has stumbled across a woodland mansion surrounded by a roofed forest and a mushroom island biome nearby. Can you help him track down the brown mooshroom?

6

TICK, TICK ... BOOM!

Bobby foolishly used all of his TNT in one go and now everything has been exploded! Can you spot Bobby, the brown mooshroom, and all his pesky foes?

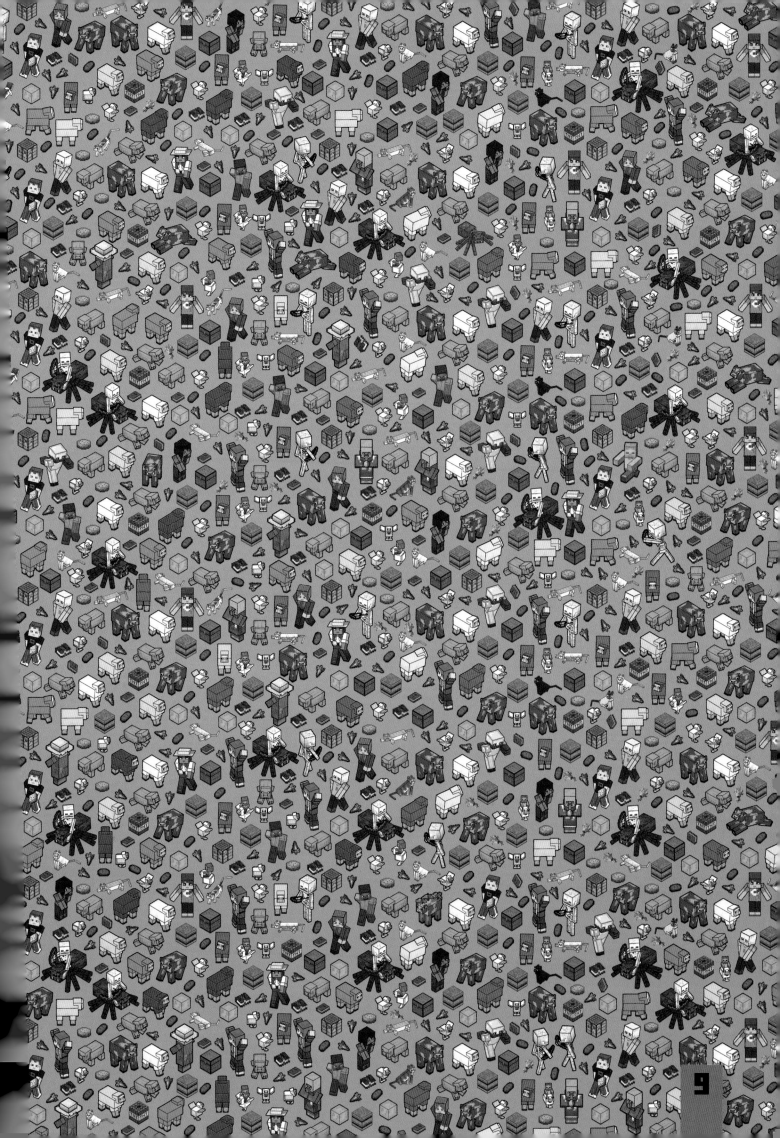

DISCOVER THE DROWNED

Idris the Impulsive only took cake and a tadpole with him on his underwater adventure.

Can you spot Idris swimming beneath the ocean? You'll need to be quick. Though tasty, cake is useless in combat, and there's a drowned lurking nearby. Spot Idris, the tropical fish variant, tadpole, and sea turtle he's searching for, plus the drowned that's after him before it's too late!

IDRIS THE IMPULSIVE

This is Idris. You might be wondering what makes him impulsive. Well, Idris doesn't believe in planning. To him, life is a big adventure and, as long as he has a cake in hand and Timmy the Tadpole for company, nothing bad can ever happen. Idris would be wrong. Many bad things can happen in the ocean, such as drowning, drowned, guardians, elder guardians, pufferfish—did I mention drowning? Oh, Idris. You silly sausage.

DROWNED

There's bound to be a drowned skulking in the depths somewhere, waiting to pounce on Idris. On the bright side, it doesn't have a trident—but as cake isn't one of its weaknesses, that's only a small comfort! Can you spot it before it spots Idris?

MEMO THE TROPICAL FISH

It's Bobby's birthday tomorrow, and Idris knows that his favorite colors are orange and white. He has decided that fetching Bobby a tropical fish in those colors would be the best present ever. How does the name Memo sound? Idris needs your help finding Memo. Can you spot it?

SEA TURTLE

Shortly after diving into the ocean depths, Idris realized that he can't breathe for very long underwater. So he set off in search of a sea turtle. But Idris had not researched sea turtles in advance. If he had, he'd know that only baby sea turtles drop scutes, when they grow into adults.

TIMMY THE TADPOLE

Idris had a good idea. He knew that tropical fish only spawn in warm or lukewarm oceans, but all the seas felt cold to him. So he thought that if he let Timmy out of his bucket, he would soon grow up. Then, if he became a white or orange frog, he'd know he was in the right ocean. What he didn't expect was for Timmy to swim away. Whoops!

GETTING SOME VITAMIN SEA

Idris has taken a deep dive beneath the ocean in search of Bobby's birthday present. Oh look! He's come across a shipwreck. Can you help him find what he's looking for?

A MONUMENT-OUS OCCASION

Idris is still searching when he locates an ocean monument! Help him find the tropical fish, a sea turtle, and Timmy the Tadpole before the drowned or guardians get him.

HUNT THE HUSK

Samiko the Survivor believes she can thrive in any biome. Let's hope she's right!

Samiko has ventured into the desert with nothing at all in her inventory—apparently she likes a challenge. Luckily, she's made it to a village before sundown. Not so luckily, zombies are invading it and the desert sunshine doesn't always mean safety. Watch out, Samiko—there's a husk about!

SAMIKO THE SURVIVOR

Samiko is a confident survivor. So confident, in fact, that before every new adventure, she empties her inventory. However, she would have been wise to stock up on at least some snacks before this journey—the desert isn't known for its abundance of food. Thankfully, she has a knack for surviving sticky situations, which is handy because she often finds herself in them!

HUSK

Zombies spawn in the desert the same as anywhere else, but unlike other biomes, not all zombies will perish when the sun rises. Some spawn as husks—a terrifying zombie variant that can survive in the daylight. Look out, Samiko! One is coming for you!

PERSIAN CAT

Samiko has decided she is a cat person. And not only that, but a Persian cat person. She really loves the color beige. She's been searching far and wide for one but with little luck, so today she decided to try a desert village.
To be fair, Persian cats are very pretty!

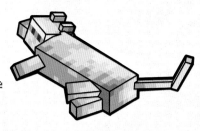

CHICKEN JOCKEY

Yay! A chicken! Samiko's food-shortage issues have been answered. Over here, Samiko! Oh wait. There's a baby zombie riding that chicken. Hide, Samiko, hide! Chickens may be tasty, but baby zombies are nasty! This is definitely a mob combo she should avoid! Can you spot it before it's too late for Samiko?

KILLER BUNNY

Watch out, Samiko! You might think that's just a regular rabbit, but it's got a nasty streak! Someone has spawned a killer bunny! If Samiko gets too close, it will leap at her and attack. Quick, can you spot its evil red eyes before it springs into action?

WE'LL NEVER DESERT YOU

Can you help Samiko spot the Persian cat without running into the killer bunny, husk, or chicken jockey? Having to sprint away from them all would be quite the task!

THE WICKED WITCH IS A PEST

Samiko was so busy finding her new pet that she didn't watch out for hostile mobs. A witch threw a splash potion at her, and finding everything just got harder! Can you help her find the Persian cat?

DETECT THE ZOMBIE VILLAGER

Carina the Curious always has her head in a book.

Oh no! Carina worked so hard to build new villages, and now they are being invaded. In the chaos, she has lost her two faithful companions: Alan the Allay and Wolfrick the Wolf. Can you help Carina find her friends, while keeping an eye out for the pesky witch and menacing zombie villager that are lurking nearby?

CARINA THE CURIOUS

Carina will do anything for a new book, including raiding structures and battling mobs for them. She's even taken to building entire villages in new biomes in an effort to get more books from villagers. She now has a huge collection for her library, but will she look up from her books long enough to see the chaos going on around her?

ZOMBIE VILLAGER

Groan! Where did that come from? Oh no, one of Carina's sweet villagers has been turned into a zombie villager! We can't just leave them that way. One of Carina's books is bound to tell her how to cure them. She just needs your help finding them first. Can you spot the poor soul?

ALAN THE ALLAY

Carina managed to liberate Alan from a cage while searching a pillager outpost for a new book. Not only is Alan mega cute, but it also brings her blocks, which is super handy. In her haste to leave the outpost, she almost forgot her new book and the ominous bottle the raid captain dropped!

WITCH

Oh dear, there's a wicked witch nearby. Quick, spot it before it sees Carina. Witches throw nasty splash potions at players, and Carina isn't looking where she's going. Seriously, Carina, stop reading, now is not the time! Argh, I can't watch. She's a sitting duck out there! You'll help her, won't you?

WOLFRICK THE WOLF

Wolfrick is with Carina wherever she goes, taking care of skeletons for her, so that she can read and walk at the same time. She'd be devastated to lose her wolf. Can you spot it?

PILLAGERS VS VILLAGERS

Carina's triggered a village raid. Now the village she spent weeks on is being invaded by pillagers! Help Carina find her friends and escape the raid alive!

DAWN OF THE WELL-READ

The villagers are holding a fair to celebrate the completion of their new village, but wait. Who is groaning? ARGH—zombies are beginning to invade! Quick, help Carina find her friends!

SPOT THE ZOMBIFIED PIGLIN

Arnold the Adventurous is on a mission to avoid zombies.

Arnold has made his home in the Nether. Sure, it's full of lava, piglins with bad tempers and a strange obsession with gold, and mobs that launch fiery missiles at you. But it doesn't have any zombies—and zombies are the WORST. And yet . . . The Nether isn't as free of zombified mobs as he first thought! Can you spot them all?

ARNOLD THE ADVENTUROUS

Say hello to Arnold. Unless you're a zombie. Arnold hates zombies. He once saw one defeat a poor, innocent baby sea turtle and decided right then that he never wanted to see a zombie ever again. The only issue is, there are a lot of zombies in the Overworld, so he decided to move to the Nether. But now there are zombified mobs here, too. Quick, shoo them back through the Nether portal before he sees them!

ZOMBIFIED PIGLIN

It looks like a silly piglin decided to go on vacation to the Overworld and didn't realize the strange effects this dimension would have on them! Unfortunately for them, zombification can't be treated, and even returning to the Nether won't cure them. Can you spot them hiding?

ZOMBIFIED PIGLIN JOCKEY

Not another zombified piglin! ARGH! And this one can cross lava! Who knew they could spawn on a strider?! Unless you have a strider saddled up and ready yourself, you're best defeating this beastly mob duo from afar!

ZOGLIN

Ooo pork! Oh wait. That isn't a hoglin. It's a zoglin! Gross. No one wants to eat that mob's rotten flesh—it could give you the Hunger effect. We'd better keep it away from Arnold.

PIG

Oh no, we missed one! Oh wait. It's just a pig. HOORAY! Look, Arnold, a source of pork that doesn't fight back. Quick, before it falls into a lava pit! Sorry, pig.

NEVER SAY NETHER

It's chaos in the Nether. What was Arnold thinking when he moved here?! Search through the bastion remnant for Arnold and keep him away from all those zombified mobs.

TAKE IT FOR A SPIN

Arnold swears he just saw a zombified piglin. But then he blinked and all he could see were piglins. He looks around. There? No. There? He spins and spins until he gets dizzy.

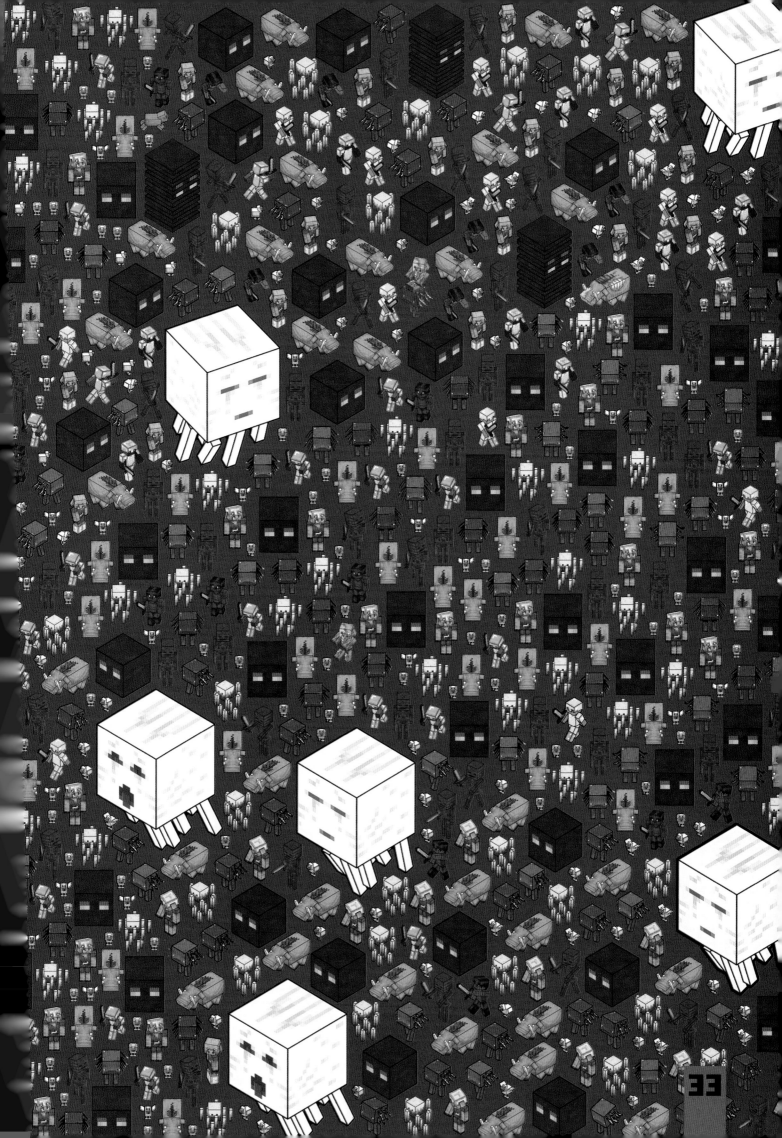

WHAT ELSE CAN YOU FIND?

Congratulations! You checked in on all of the explorers! Were you able to help them out?

You must be an incredible explorer to have found everyone and survived to tell the tale! And what stories they must be. No? Well, what were you looking at? I bet there are loads of things you missed! Why don't you go back and refresh your memory. See if you can find all these bonus items.

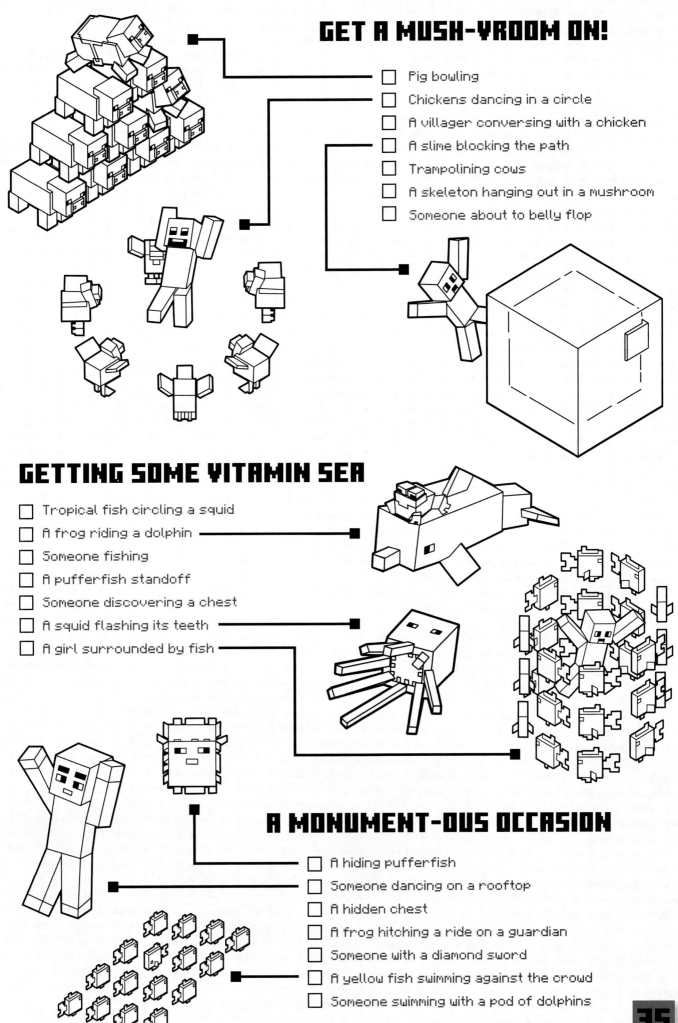

GET A MUSH-VROOM ON!

- [ ] Pig bowling
- [ ] Chickens dancing in a circle
- [ ] A villager conversing with a chicken
- [ ] A slime blocking the path
- [ ] Trampolining cows
- [ ] A skeleton hanging out in a mushroom
- [ ] Someone about to belly flop

GETTING SOME VITAMIN SEA

- [ ] Tropical fish circling a squid
- [ ] A frog riding a dolphin
- [ ] Someone fishing
- [ ] A pufferfish standoff
- [ ] Someone discovering a chest
- [ ] A squid flashing its teeth
- [ ] A girl surrounded by fish

A MONUMENT-OUS OCCASION

- [ ] A hiding pufferfish
- [ ] Someone dancing on a rooftop
- [ ] A hidden chest
- [ ] A frog hitching a ride on a guardian
- [ ] Someone with a diamond sword
- [ ] A yellow fish swimming against the crowd
- [ ] Someone swimming with a pod of dolphins

WE'LL NEVER DESERT YOU

- [ ] An Enderman stealing a cat
- [ ] Someone being trampled by sheep
- [ ] A suspicious gathering of five creepers
- [ ] An iron golem exchanging flowers with a player
- [ ] People building a sandcastle
- [ ] Someone wearing a Jack O'Lantern on their head
- [ ] A rabbit contemplating whether it can swim in lava

PILLAGERS VS VILLAGERS

- [ ] Someone tickling a pillager with a feather
- [ ] A chicken throwing eggs
- [ ] A pillager captain shouting orders
- [ ] An iron golem assembling its sheep army
- [ ] A flying steak
- [ ] Someone gorging on an entire melon
- [ ] Cats rounding up a group of creepers

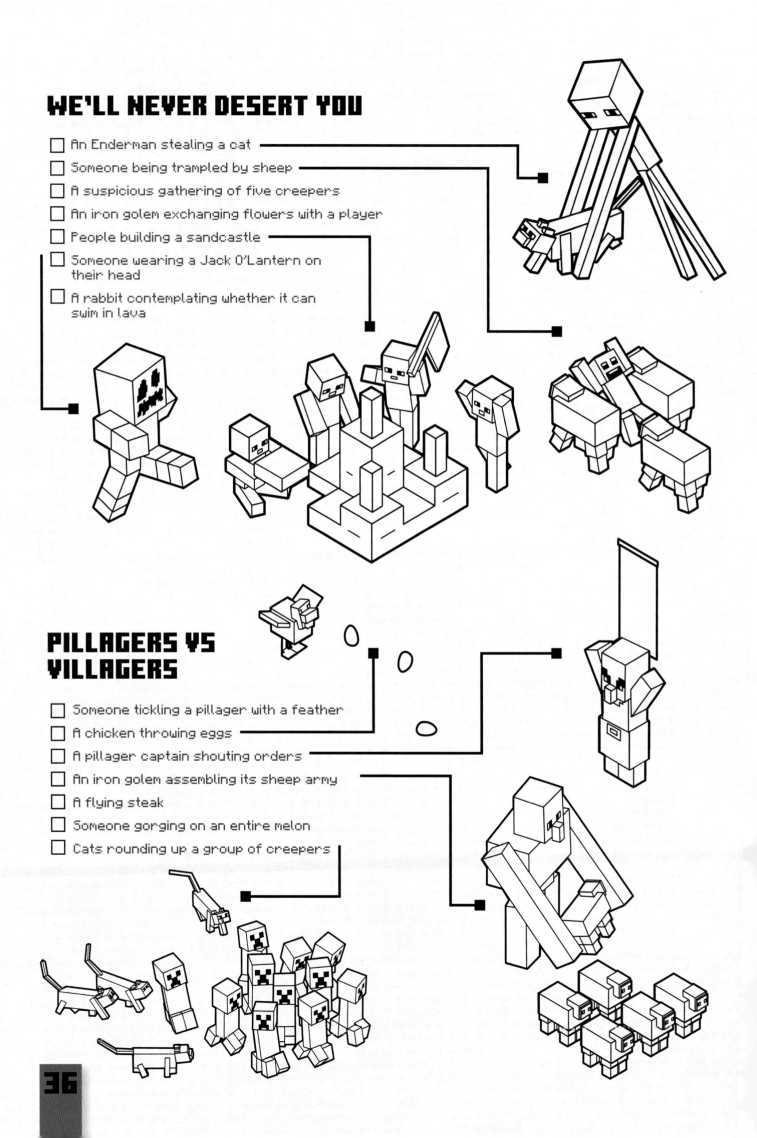

DAWN OF THE WELL-READ

- [ ] A villager wedding
- [ ] Someone selling the Master Builds book
- [ ] Chickens playing in the fountain
- [ ] Someone telling a riveting story
- [ ] Two fools stealing beehives
- [ ] A frog pool party
- [ ] Someone riding a pig into battle

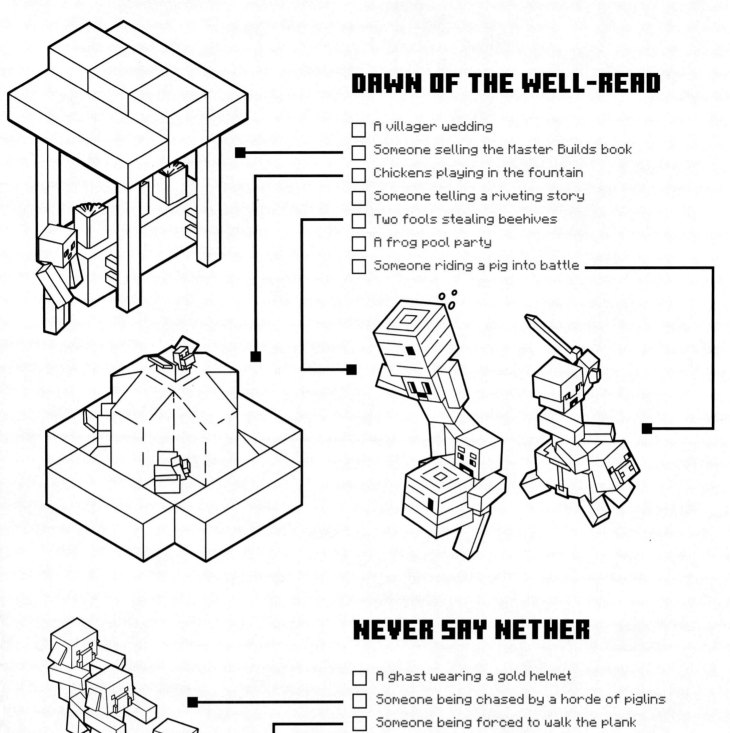

NEVER SAY NETHER

- [ ] A ghast wearing a gold helmet
- [ ] Someone being chased by a horde of piglins
- [ ] Someone being forced to walk the plank
- [ ] A chicken having a lava bath
- [ ] A chicken riding a ghast
- [ ] A horse no doubt regretting its decision to follow its owner through the Nether portal
- [ ] Two people playing a dangerous game of chicken fight on striders

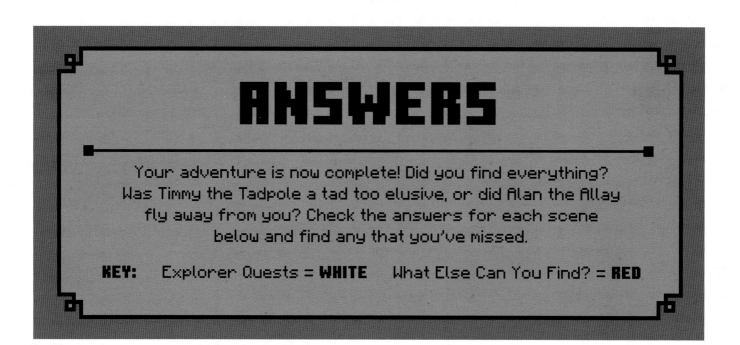

ANSWERS

Your adventure is now complete! Did you find everything?
Was Timmy the Tadpole a tad too elusive, or did Alan the Allay
fly away from you? Check the answers for each scene
below and find any that you've missed.

KEY: Explorer Quests = **WHITE**   What Else Can You Find? = **RED**

FIND THE ZOMBIE

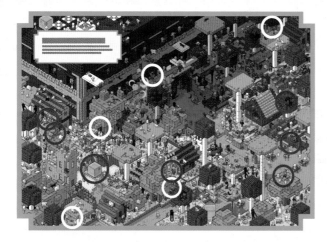

GET A MUSH-VROOM ON

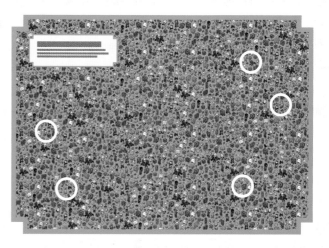

TICK, TICK ... BOOM!

DISCOVER THE DROWNED

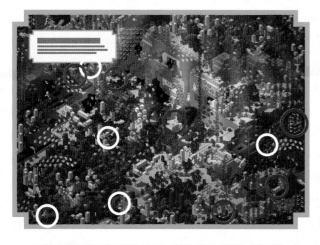

GETTING SOME VITAMIN SEA

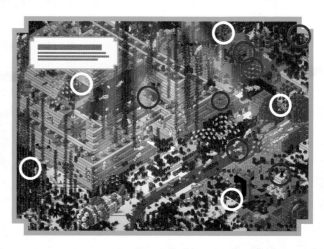

A MONUMENT-OUS OCCASION

HUNT THE HUSK

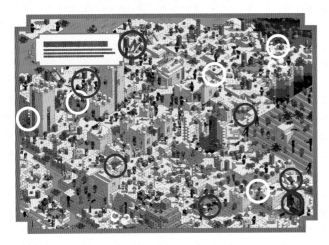

WE'LL NEVER DESERT YOU

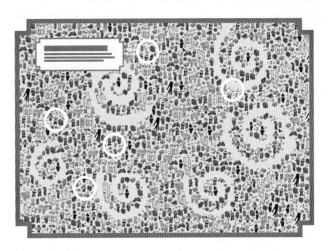

THE WICKED WITCH IS A PEST

DETECT THE ZOMBIE VILLAGER

PILLAGERS VS VILLAGERS

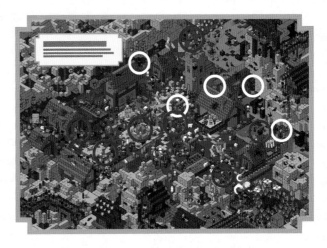

DAWN OF THE WELL-READ

SPOT THE ZOMBIFIED PIGLIN

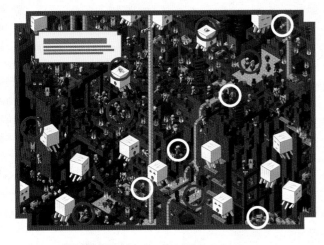

NEVER SAY NETHER

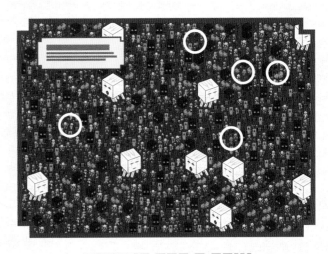

TAKE IT FOR A SPIN

GOTCHA!